SHADOWCATS

Shadowcats

by

Anna Taborska

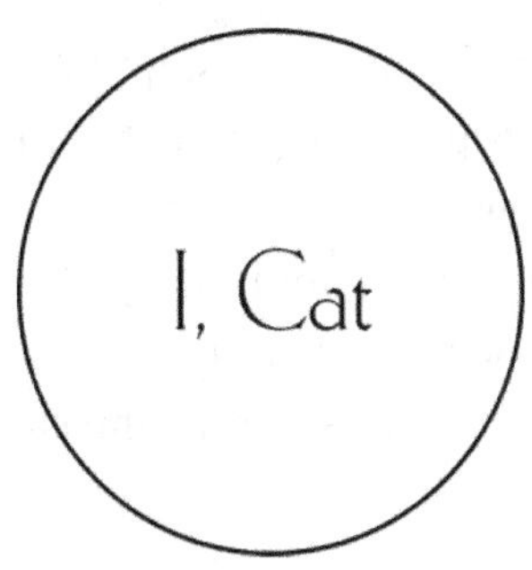

ancient deity curled on your sofa
all soft fur and soporific gaze
I suffer your company
and accept the food you offer
that I might sheathe my claws
and spare the wildlife in your yard

sunlight veils my darker nature
but the night whispers my name
and a myriad stars reflect
in my eyes as old as sin
life holds no surprises for me
– nor death –
for I have tasted blood
and immortality

the pharaohs worshipped me
the ignorant persecuted me
now you take my feral spirit
for a place by your meagre hearth
but you will never tap my wisdom
nor touch my age-old mystery

The Cat Sitter

At fifteen acres, the wood wasn't particularly large, but the brooding, oppressive atmosphere, which so belied the usual beauty of ancient English woodland, gave it an air of menace infinitely vaster than its physical area. If an unwary rambler, caught up amongst what should have been a splendid array of native trees, were to analyse why he or she felt unease rather than tranquillity amongst the leafy bowers of Ash Wood, here's what they might conclude...

The wood was darker than it should have been. True, the centuries-old trees that formed it grew tall and dense, but the permanent gloom that appeared to rest upon Ash Wood contravened the laws of light and shadow. The twigs and branches of its trees creaked and rattled like dry bones. Leaves were parched brown. Flowers, on the rare occasions that they bloomed, grew dried and shrivelled on their desiccated stalks. It defied logic how, even when the surrounding area became waterlogged after heavy rains, the soil in the wood remained dry and cracked. The more imaginative visitor might surmise that it was as if the very earth of the wood smouldered with an insatiable ire that sucked the nurturing moisture out of anything that tried to flourish within it.

Shadows flitted uneasily amongst the trees, and the undergrowth rustled with a wrathful air of impatience. And yet no animals ventured into the wood to account for these phenomena. There was no birdsong either, as living things seemed to shun Ash Wood and skirted fearfully around its perimeter, preferring instead to purloin a bit of greenery, an earthworm or a sip of water from the cottage garden that backed onto the wood.

~

Thursday 27th April

Jane was excited at the prospect of seeing Isabelle's new house, and of seeing her old friend again. The last time they'd met was at a friend's wedding in Denmark, and that was well over a year ago. Even the long drive to Sussex, the surprisingly heavy traffic and the frustration of getting lost a couple of times on ridiculously narrow country lanes didn't dampen Jane's enthusiasm.

Jane and Isabelle had both studied at St Hilda's College, Oxford. Isabelle had finished her English studies after three years and moved to London, where she'd worked in retail for eight years before meeting and marrying Jonathan. Jane's degree in Human Sciences had stretched to four years – the result of her third year consisting of a ten-month placement at a prestigious American university. After finishing her degree Jane had moved back to Manchester and the two girls had lost touch, only reconnecting via social media years later.

The houses along the country lanes became fewer and fewer, and finally dwindled away to the odd farmhouse. Soon these too disappeared, leaving only vast stretches of farmland, punctuated by the occasional derelict outbuilding or disused barn. Isabelle had explained that she'd had enough of London, and couldn't wait to buy a house with Jonathan in the countryside and take her fledgling internet retail business to 'the next level'. Her dream had finally come true when the estate agent managed to procure a cottage on the outskirts of Wraithsfield – a small village in East Sussex. Jonathan could still commute into London three times a week, Isabelle could travel into the capital too when absolutely necessary, but other than that they could live the country idyll – along with Milly the cat.

Jonathan hadn't wanted a cat. He was sure that it would wreak havoc with the rabbits, squirrels, birds and other gentle wildlife that frequented the back garden of Ash Wood Cottage, and he was right. But Isabelle – a robust and unsentimental lass if ever there was one – had little sympathy for anything that couldn't cope with a bit of Darwinian selection (albeit not of a very natural origin), and insisted that she wanted an animal to keep her company inside the house – not just ones that gate-crashed her garden and fled as soon as they caught wind of her. And Jonathan certainly wasn't going to let a few dead bunnies stand between his beloved and her happiness. So Milly the cat was promptly purchased and named, and now constituted the perfect excuse for Jane to come and visit her old friend's new house.

More country lanes, fringed on either side with claustrophobic, impenetrable hedges. Then these too gave way to an open vista of sizeable fields, empty save for the odd cow, and finally Jane passed a small lane leading off the road to a white-walled two-storey cottage. She brought the car to a halt, made sure the deserted road was still deserted, executed a somewhat clumsy three-point turn and doubled-back, turning up the lane leading to the cottage. She parked alongside her hosts' gleaming SUV and got out of her battered old Peugeot, relieved to be out in the fresh air and stretching her legs and back. She took her small suitcase out of the boot, locked the car, and headed for the house.

"Jane!" Isabelle had spotted her through the window and was beaming at her from the doorstep. "You're here!"

"No thanks to the traffic." Jane put down her suitcase and embraced her friend.

"Let me take that!" Jonathan appeared from behind Isabelle, gave Jane a hug and carried her suitcase into the house.

Ash Wood Cottage was a curious mixture of the very old and the very new. The estate agent had told Jonathan and Isabelle that some parts of the cottage originally dated back to the seventeenth century, but even those parts had been obscured by centuries of renovations and 'improvements'. Now the cottage boasted a fitted kitchen with fully integrated appliances, two double bedrooms, a bathroom with a power shower, and a spacious sitting room. On one side the sitting room opened onto a dining room; on the opposite side and in the far wall, it had two large double-glazed windows that met at right angles to form a vast frameless corner window overlooking the pretty garden and the wood beyond. The entrance to the cottage was at the side of the building, leading directly into the kitchen.

Jonathan carried Jane's bag up to the spare bedroom, while Isabelle took her on a tour and showed her where she could find kitchen utensils, Milly's cat food, replacement cat litter and anything else she might need during Jonathan and Isabelle's long weekend in Spain.

"I guess it's time you met Milly," said Isabelle. "I expect she's in the garden as usual. Shall we have a quick look?" Jane nodded enthusiastically and they went outdoors.

Isabelle was somewhat miffed by the fact that Milly spent such a great deal of time in the garden. What was the point of having a pet that was meant to keep her company indoors when said pet spent much of the day outdoors, staring into the wood at the back of the house, only to come fearfully inside at night when the shadows among the trees got too much for her? Isabelle had all the downsides of owning a pet – scratched furniture, decapitated bunnies, dead birds and bleeding field mice – without the companionship that she'd anticipated when Jonathan was away and she sat at her computer alone. But still, when Milly did venture in, she followed Isabelle around, purring at her, rubbing up against her legs, allowing herself to be stroked and obligingly chasing the piece of string that her mistress sometimes dangled in front of her. *No such thing as the perfect pet* thought Isabelle, as she led her friend across the small patio and up three stone steps to the overgrown lawn.

"Milly!" The cat had been standing at the far end of the lawn, gazing into the woods, and now turned to look in the direction of the two women. "Come and meet Jane!" Milly trotted over to Isabelle and allowed herself to be picked up and stroked. "This is Jane." Isabelle turned the cat to face her friend. "She's going to look after you."

"She's beautiful." Jane reached out to stroke Milly, but the cat meowed loudly in protest, wriggled out of Isabelle's grasp and ran off.

"Oh, sorry about that," said Isabelle. "It takes her a little while to get used to people she doesn't know. She'll be fine in an hour or so."

"It's alright." Jane smiled shyly, doing her best to hide her disappointment at the rejection by her furry charge.

Dear Jane thought Isabelle, *sweet, sensitive, chubby Jane, with her little round spectacles and her mild manners. Even the cat has a stronger personality than she does.*

"Come on, let's go have some tea," suggested Isabelle, and headed back towards the house. As Jane turned to follow, she thought she heard someone whisper her name. She glanced back at the woods, startled and a little afraid, but it was only the wind sighing in the dry branches.

Jane never slept well in an unfamiliar place, and that night was no exception. She, Jonathan and Isabelle had stayed up chatting for a while after dinner, but her hosts had an early start the following day, so the three of them retired early. The spare bedroom had been turned into a study for Isabelle, but it doubled as a guestroom and contained a single bed. As Jane draped her clothes over the armchair in the corner, she caught a whiff of a strange smell – faint, but unpleasant nonetheless. Then it was gone.

Jane read for a little while, then tossed and turned for a long while, then fell asleep, only to dream about the dark expanse of wood behind the cottage. She was standing on the lawn, peering into the trees in a vain attempt to see who it was that had called her name. Her unease grew as she noticed shadows moving among the trees, and she decided to return to the cottage. She tried to move, but found that she was rooted to the spot. She was forced to watch as the shadows danced and swayed, merging with each other and congealing into a single vast darkness. As tendrils of black mist spilled forward, reaching for Jane, the anxiety levels in her sleeping body soared enough to wake her up.

The particulars of her dream faded quickly, but a sense of disquiet lingered long enough for her to switch on the bedside lamp and read some more before attempting to go back to sleep.

~

Friday 28th April

In the morning Jane got up early to wave her friends goodbye and feed the cat. Milly purred while Jane opened a tin of cat food and scooped it out into a plastic bowl, but shied away the moment Jane tried to stroke her. She wolfed down her food and immediately demanded to be let out. Jane obliged, then went back to bed to try to make up for her poor night's sleep. There was definitely a stale smell in her room, and Jane wondered absentmindedly whether her friends' dream house had damp, before dozing off for a couple of hours.

After a late breakfast – brunch really – Jane decided to check on the cat and go for a walk. It was a sunny day and Milly was lying in the long grass in the garden, eyes fixed on the wood beyond the lawn. Jane admired the cat's unusual calico colouring – black and ginger patches all over, with a white belly, collar and socks. But strangest of all was Milly's face – half of it black with black whiskers and a yellow eye, the other half ginger with white whiskers and a blue eye. If that wasn't quirky enough, the rim of Milly's black ear was tinged with ginger, while her ginger ear was similarly tinged with black. And the cat's ears were pointed and tufty, giving her an altogether somewhat demonic appearance.

Milly didn't move as Jane walked past her, neither did she follow as Jane stepped over the fallen single-wire fence and headed off into the woods. She stared after the departing woman, still as a sphinx, and only her twitching tail gave away her agitation at the cat sitter's disappearance into the wilderness that both fascinated and frightened her.

Ash Wood would have been beautiful, thought Jane, if only the trees and bushes didn't look so unhealthy. There was nothing wrong with them really, apart from the fact that they seemed dehydrated. Odd, considering that it had been a rather wet April. But even in its current state, the wood impressed with its wide variety of deciduous trees and a few evergreens to boot. Jane knew a little about trees – she made

a point of knowing a little about everything –
and there was one thing that puzzled her. She
had spied alder, willow, oak, yew, aspen,
hawthorn, birch, holly and hornbeam, but there
was not an ash tree in sight. And yet the wood
was named Ash Wood.

As she headed further into the wilderness,
Jane kept her eyes peeled for the eponymous ash
trees, and in the end spotted three – in a wood
of thousands of trees. She knew that place
names often made little sense, but for some
reason the discrepancy bothered her. She sat
down for a while on the trunk of a fallen oak and
listened to the profound silence around her. The
absence of birdsong was strange, the lack of any
evidence of wildlife surprising, and Jane
wondered whether a harmful chemical had been
dumped or buried in the soil.

As she sat and pondered, Jane's mind
unexpectedly went blank, as if her train of
thought had been cut off abruptly. As she
struggled with the sudden disorientation, her
ears started to ring – a low, hollow sound. Then
something seemed to be pushing at the edges of
Jane's consciousness, like an icy tentacle
reaching its way inside her head, probing her

mind, displacing her thoughts. Jane tried to pull herself together, she tried to focus on something – anything – but she couldn't get a mental foothold and she started to lose her sense of where she ended and the wood began. She battled to get a grip on herself, but the ringing in her ears had become a sickening rhythmic chanting, and it was intensifying, preventing her from hearing her own thoughts.

"No!" With a supreme effort Jane regained control and snapped out of the disembodying, trancelike state. The ringing in her ears was gone. She leapt up and ran through the woods back to the cottage.

Milly, who was still lying in the same spot on the lawn, started as Jane ran past her.

As Jane opened the front door, she noticed that the telephone was ringing. She had no strength left to run, but moved as swiftly as she could to the sitting-room and picked up the receiver.

"Hello?"

"Jane?" It was Isabelle. "Are you okay?"

"I was outside."

"Oh, sorry I dragged you in." Isabelle relaxed a little, putting Jane's strained panting down to having run for the phone. "You better get your breath back."

"I'm okay."

"Good. How's Milly?"

"She's fine. She's in the garden. I'm going to give her some biscuits soon."

"Thanks a lot, Jane. I really appreciate your help. Jonathan and I really need this."

Jane spent the rest of the day indoors. She couldn't understand what had happened in the woods. Could it have been a psychotic episode? An indicator of the early onset of some kind of dissociative disorder? Schizophrenia perhaps? But there was no mental illness in her family, and an attack like this, with no previous hint of disease, made little sense. She'd been looking forward to spending the bank holiday enjoying the sunshine, but now she felt reluctant to leave the house. Confinement within the four walls of the cottage made her feel less vulnerable. Besides, it would be getting dark soon, and she certainly had no wish to go out after dark. But she didn't want Milly to stay out after nightfall either. Isabelle would never forgive her, and she'd never forgive herself, if something happened to Milly on her watch. She'd have to bring the cat back in and she'd have to do it soon.

When Jane finally plucked up the courage to go out, she skirted along the wall of the house until she reached the corner, where the patio began. She craned her neck but couldn't see the cat, so she eventually scaled the steps that led up to the lawn and peered reluctantly in the direction of the wood. Sure enough, Milly was there – sitting at the far end of the lawn and gaping into the wood as though she was drawn to it, yet feared to set paw in it at the same time.

"Milly!" The cat turned her head to look at Jane, but didn't move. "Milly, come on! Come here! Good kitty!" Nothing. After a while Milly turned her head back towards the trees and ignored Jane's further entreaties altogether. Jane couldn't bear to cross the lawn. She thought for a minute, then headed back to the house, emerging moments later with a box of cat biscuits, which she rattled enticingly. Milly perked up.

"Come on, Milly! Biscuit time! Here, kitty, kitty!" Jane shook the box once more and this time it did the trick. Milly stood up slowly, stretched, then walked in a slow and dignified manner towards Jane, finally following her into the house.

Jane locked the door behind them. She was grateful to have Milly's company and found the crunching sound of her devouring the dry cat food somehow soothing. She ventured to stroke Milly again and this time the cat didn't flinch. Jane smiled as Milly purred and arched her back beneath Jane's hand. She made sure that the doors and windows were locked, and the two of them watched television together – Milly in Jonathan's chair and Jane on the sofa.

There were no curtains or blinds in the sitting-room – either because Jonathan and Isabelle didn't feel the need for them (there were no neighbours to look in from the back of the house) or because they simply hadn't got round to putting any up. Either way, Jane consciously avoided looking out of the window as the woods beyond the lawn darkened and shadows moved among the trees. When night fell fully, Jane couldn't shake the feeling that she was being watched, so she switched everything off and went upstairs to bed. There was that faint, irritating smell in her room again, but she felt mentally and physically drained, and soon fell asleep.

A sharp meow woke her up. She was standing at the front door, hand on the door handle, Milly gazing up at her and meowing in alarm. Jane cried out in distress, and Milly ran out of the kitchen. As the shock wore off and Jane's heartbeat returned to normal, she noticed how cold her feet were on the stone-flagged kitchen floor. She made sure the entrance door was still locked, put on the kettle, and went upstairs to don her slippers and a dressing-gown.

Back in the kitchen, Jane tried to analyse the day's events rationally. She had never sleepwalked before and she'd never had a dissociative episode. Then again, she'd never been on her own in such an isolated place. There was something eldritch about the secluded cottage and the strange, withered wood that all but surrounded it. And it was in the wood that Jane believed the key to the mystery of her unprecedented episodes lay. She thought back to the dry, parched earth, the desiccated plant life and lack of animal life, and the disturbing notion that the land might be chemically poisoned or otherwise toxic resurfaced in her mind. That would explain her auditory hallucination and her sudden disorientation; perhaps the sleepwalking as well.

But if there was something toxic in the ground, then how come nobody seemed to know about it? She'd have to tell Isabelle and Jonathan. She didn't want to spoil their pastoral idyll, but she'd have to share her suspicions with them. Isabelle would be gutted. The thought of being the harbinger of bad news upset Jane.

Milly wandered back into the kitchen, and Jane decided to spoil her by topping up her cat biscuits. She watched as the cat crunched voraciously, and drank her own hot chocolate slowly, returning to bed only when the dawn chorus started up outside.

~

Saturday 29th April

Jane woke to the sound of meowing outside her bedroom door. She fed Milly and hesitantly let her out into the garden, leaving the front door open for her. As she returned to her room to dress, she got a strong waft of the unpleasant smell. It was pungent and rather nasty. Jane had a quick look around the room, but didn't see anything untoward. She opened the window before going back to the kitchen to make her breakfast. To her surprise, Milly was sitting on the floor by the sofa, looking up at her expectantly as Jane walked in with a cup of tea.

"Hello, Milly," said Jane, settling down on the sofa. As soon as she sat down, Jane jumped up again in surprise, spilling her tea on the cream-colored rug. "Oh my God!"

She stared down at the soft, sticky thing she'd squashed when she sat down. It was a dead field mouse, blood still oozing from it onto the sofa. "Oh, Milly... you got me a present." Jane looked down at the cat in exasperation. Milly was purring loudly, tail weaving slowly from side to side on the rug, waiting to see whether the gift she'd procured for her new friend and placed on her spot on the sofa would be appreciated.

"You shouldn't have," Jane told the cat. "I mean, you *really* shouldn't have." Milly came over and rubbed herself against Jane's leg. Jane stroked her briefly before setting about removing the little corpse, cleaning the tea off the rug and washing the blood off the leather sofa and the seat of her trousers.

The rest of the day passed uneventfully. Milly was back outside, staring at the woods. The weather was good and for a moment Jane felt relaxed enough to contemplate going for a walk, but the incident in the woods still haunted her and she decided to remain indoors. She remembered the horrible ringing in her ears – the pulsing, stupor-inducing humming, like the chanting of people in some kind of trance – and the lower-pitched, darker, unfamiliar and altogether more menacing sound behind it. An image insinuated itself into Jane's mind – a horrible half-glimpsed image from the past that she'd tried hard to forget.

During her third year at Oxford, Jane had travelled to the United States as an exchange student. Her tutor, Dr Cornelius Bainbridge, had a fascination with books of ancient lore – a fact he kept quiet from the rest of the Human Sciences Department, as such things were frowned upon among the dreaming spires. Bainbridge had always wanted to spend some time studying the rarer occult tomes housed in the famed library at the Miskatonic University in Arkham, Massachusetts, but he'd already spent his sabbatical perusing archaic Sumerian texts in the Middle East, so he devised the cunning plan of arranging an exchange between some of the most gifted students from his department and students from the Miskatonic's Anthropology Department. Fortuitously for Bainbridge, the Department Head at the Miskatonic, Professor William Freeborn (great nephew, as it happened, of the late Tyler M. Freeborn – valued Professor at the same Department in the 1930s), harboured an almost obsessive desire to get his hands on the notorious *Liber Tenebrarum*, the original and last surviving copy of which was purported to be held in the vast labyrinthine stacks of the Bodleian Library in Oxford. The two academics managed to persuade their respective universities to agree to the exchange, which Bainbridge and Freeborn of course insisted on overseeing personally.

Jane was one of only five students from Oxford to have been selected. Dr Bainbridge had a lot of time for the ungainly, introverted girl because of her higher than average intelligence, superior reasoning skills, tenacious mind and protestant work ethic. And so, when Jane expressed an interest in his work, Bainbridge arranged permission for her to accompany him on one of his research days. Staff at the Miskatonic objected on the grounds that their own undergraduates were not permitted to access the most famous artefacts in the library's occult collection – not just on account of their age and concomitant fragility, but also due to the effect that studying their contents might have on young and impressionable minds prone to flights of fancy. Bainbridge had vouched for Jane's good sense in handling precious and delicate documents, and for her sensible and healthily sceptical attitude towards any reading matter she might encounter. And so Jane was allowed to view the Miskatonic's most treasured volumes of arcane literature under the supervision of her tutor.

The two of them were ushered to a restricted room within the library, where Bainbridge had free access to such dread marvels as von Junzt's *Unaussprechlichen Kulten*, the mysterious and fragmentary *Book of Eibon*, and perhaps the most infamous of the library's collection – Abdul Alhazred's *Al Azif*, better known by its Greek name: *Necronomicon*. It was in the *Necronomicon* that Jane had caught a fleeting glimpse of an illustration depicting shadowy figures performing an ancient rite; a fleeting glimpse because at that moment Jane's vision blurred, her ears started to ring and a sharp, thumping pain erupted inside her head, resulting in her first ever migraine. Dr Bainbridge commented that it must have been the culmination of hours spent poring over musty books in a dusty, ill-ventilated room, and he was probably right, as after a drink of water, plenty of fresh air and a good night's sleep, Jane felt considerably better.

Funny that she'd forgotten all about the ringing in her ears that had preceded the migraine – the ringing she'd heard again in the forest before her episode. She hoped she wasn't going to have another migraine, although in a way that might be preferable to the terrifying blackout or panic attack she'd experienced yesterday. She hadn't seen the horrid illustration clearly on that day in the Miskatonic library, and even now, it was more a feeling of cosmic dread that suffused her memory than a clear recollection of anything she might have seen.

Jane distracted herself by watching daytime TV and reading. Once or twice she peered outside to see if she could spy Milly in the long grass, but the cat was probably on the far side of the lawn, which wasn't visible from the sitting-room window. In the end she'd deemed it best to keep the front door locked, and opened it only occasionally to check if Milly were sitting there, waiting to be let in. She wasn't. When the sun started to set, Jane took the box of cat biscuits and braved the outside world.

"Milly! Here, kitty! Biscuit time!" But there was no response.

Jane climbed the steps from the patio to the lawn, but there was no sign of Milly. She rattled the dry cat food once more.

"Milly! Here, kitty, kitty!" Silence. Then a troubled meow from somewhere up ahead. "Milly!" Jane hesitated for a moment longer, then headed off across the lawn, alternately shaking the cat biscuit box and calling out. But there was no further response.

Jane slowed as she neared the end of the garden. She called out again, and this time was rewarded with a small, plaintive mew just ahead of her, in the unmown grass by the fallen wire fence demarcating the boundary between the garden and Ash Wood beyond. Then cat biscuits were spilling on the lawn as the box slipped from her grasp. Her ears rang with the stupefying, ominous, primal chant – like the rhythmic pounding of a giant black heart or the pulsing of a dark star on the far side of the cosmos. She was paralysed with fear, unable to scream as a will stronger than her own forced its way into her mind. Her thoughts were fragmenting, dissipating; her very essence was being forced from her body into the chill evening air. Then something bumped against her leg, and an urgent feline yowl burst through the veil that was descending upon Jane, breaking the spell, bringing her back. She was Jane once more and she was screaming. She scooped Milly up in her arms and ran back to the cottage.

Once they were through the front door, Milly tore herself from Jane's grasp and fled into the house. As Jane locked the front door and turned to follow the cat, she caught sight of the calendar hanging on the wall. 29th April. 30th tomorrow – May Eve. Walpurgis Night. One of the four major feast days celebrated by witches, second only to Hallowe'en. An ancient day of power when magic and dark ritual were at their most potent. Jane chastised herself for these silly associations, but then the hazy image from the *Necronomicon* flared in her mind once more. Obscure, silhouetted figures enacting something pre-Christian, pre-pagan; some ageless ritual pre-anything known to modern man... but to what purpose? And what did this have to do with her current situation?

Jane went around the house making sure all the windows were closed, although she hesitated before shutting the one in her bedroom. It had been a warm day and, despite the open window, the foul smell in Jane's room persisted. But she felt safer with the window closed.

Jane wanted to phone Isabelle and tell her that she couldn't stay any longer. She brought up Isabelle's mobile number, but couldn't face the conversation that would doubtless follow – the concern in her friend's voice, the questions. She'd leave food and water for Milly and lock her in the house. Isabelle and Jonathan would be back the day after tomorrow. She'd leave them a note, apologising; she'd try to explain. But what exactly would she say? And how could she leave Milly? As if by some feline sixth sense, Milly, who'd been hiding in a secret place unbeknown to anyone but her, appeared by Jane and placed her head under Jane's hand, looking up at the woman and meowing.

"Oh, Milly," said Jane, stroking the cat's head. "I messed up with your biscuits, but you can have some *Whiskas* tonight by way of an exception. Okay?" Jane fed the cat and they watched television together. This time Milly sat on the sofa next to Jane, watching her intently with, it seemed to Jane, a concerned expression in her blue and yellow eyes. The result of such close heterochromic scrutiny was a little disconcerting, but Jane gleaned some comfort from Milly's presence, and was grateful for their developing friendship. One more night after this one, and then Isabelle and Jonathan would be back and she'd be out of there.

Jane was gradually drifting off, despite the fetid odour she'd been forced to seal in with herself due to her unwillingness to sleep with the window open – not least because of yesterday's sleepwalking episode. After another sunny day, the smell was definitely worse, suggesting that it probably wasn't damp. It was probably food that had been allowed to rot – but where was it?

Jane would have to look for it in the morning. Now all she wanted to do was sleep.

She woke up on the lawn. She'd been headed for the woods, but in her stupor she'd walked right into the pile of spilt cat biscuits, and the sharp unnatural scratch of the things against her bare feet had brought her out of her trance. She stood for a moment, not knowing where or who she was. Someone in the woods was whispering her name. A wind whipped up from nowhere, and with it came the ringing, the otherworldly chanting, and Jane started to move forward again – the pull of a powerful alien will forcing her on. But Jane was wide awake now, and fighting with all her might. Milly was behind her, crying in the long grass – a plaintive howl of feline protest and fear like nothing Jane had heard before. She focused all of her dissipating being on that cry of distress behind her, and, with a supreme effort that felt like moving through quicksand, she turned and ran back towards the house. She was vaguely aware of Milly leaping through the grass ahead of her, and of the rush of cold, biting, hissing air that followed her. Then she and Milly were in the cottage, and Jane was locking the door once more.

Jane was shaking as she made herself a strong cup of coffee. She wasn't going to sleep again as long as she was in the cottage. Milly wouldn't leave her side and followed her everywhere, finally settling down on the sofa right by her sitter. Jane flicked through the channels until she found a romantic comedy. She normally hated those things, but tonight the inane, trite stupidity would hopefully wind her up enough to keep her awake.

Milly pressed herself against Jane's thigh, her little heart beating rapidly. When Jane went to the bathroom, or to the kitchen to make another cup of coffee, Milly went with her, disparate eyes following every move the sitter made.

Each time she caught herself drifting off, Jane would pinch herself or bite her own hand or go for a walk around the house. She had put chairs in front of the windows in the sitting-room and piled them up high enough with blankets to block out the view of the garden and the wood. By morning, Jane was exhausted, bewildered, shaky, but still awake.

Sunday 30th April (May Eve – Walpurgis Night)

Jittery and fragile, Jane went to her room for a fresh change of clothes. It had been a warm night, and the stench hit her full force. She ran to the bathroom and threw up all the coffee she'd spent the night drinking. When she had nothing left in her stomach, she returned to her room and searched it top to bottom. From time to time she paused, the reek of what she was now convinced was decomposing organic matter threatening to make her sick once more. Milly joined her, watching from the doorway as Jane searched in the bin, looked under the bed, opened drawers and cupboards. Her nose kept leading her to a corner of the room, but there was nothing there except the armchair. Jane grabbed the armchair by the arms and yanked it away from the wall. The sight that greeted her made her grateful that she had nothing left to throw up.

"Oh, Milly." The cat had obviously crawled right under the armchair with the decapitated rabbit and stuffed it in at the far end, against the wall, a day or two before Jane's arrival. It was well concealed – no wonder it hadn't been spotted before.

Jane was weak and disorientated. She had to remove the festering headless bunny, but she wasn't going outside. Milly watched with some interest as Jane opened the window, picked up the rabbit by its back paws and threw it out, trying not to hear the sound it made as it connected with the paving stones beneath. Then she closed the window again and changed her clothes.

Jane was amazed at how just one partial night of sleep deprivation could have such a major effect. She found she had to concentrate on every little thing she did, and pay extra attention when doing things such as making tea, as objects seemed to slip through her fingers if she didn't take the utmost care with them. She kept glancing back at the calendar in the kitchen. It was Walpurgis Night. Witches, Satanists and other cultists would be performing all kinds of bizarre rituals tonight and, although she didn't believe in the magical effects of such things, it did mean that there might be some unsavoury people out and about tonight, intent on making mischief. The kind of people who occasionally amused themselves by torturing and killing domestic pets. Milly meowed and scratched at the front door, but Jane wasn't going to let her out today.

At lunchtime Isabelle phoned. The exhaustion and wariness in Jane's voice caught her by surprise.

"Jane? Are you okay?"

"Why is it called Ash Wood?"

"Excuse me?"

"There are practically no ash trees in it. So why is it called Ash Wood?" The bizarre question and the distracted, haunted quality of Jane's voice alarmed Isabelle.

"A witch's ashes were scattered in it... Jane...? You still there?"

"I'm here. What do you mean, a witch's ashes were scattered in it?"

"Look, now's not the best time. I'll tell you the whole story when we get home."

"Tell me now. Please."

"It's just a stupid story. I don't know all the details."

"Please, Isabelle."

"All I know is that in the seventeenth century a woman who lived in the cottage was accused of bewitching a couple of men in the village, including the priest. And the villagers blamed her for the disappearances of several children. She was burnt at the stake and her ashes were scattered in the wood."

"Where in the wood?"

"I don't know. All over, I guess. Anyway, it's probably not even true. It's just a story an old man told me in the pub... Why is this so important to you?"

"You should have told me."

"Jane, don't be silly. Look, we're back tomorrow. We'll talk then. Okay?"

By teatime Jane was suffering from microsleeps. She'd catch herself nodding off for a moment, and each time it happened she came to in a state of abject fear. Sometimes, for the second that she was asleep, she thought she could hear the eerie chanting. She hated herself for ignoring Milly's begging and crying to be let out of the house. When the sun set and the shadows lengthened, Milly stopped her entreaties and peered fearfully out of the sitting room window, over the blanket that had partially slipped to reveal the woods outside.

Jane was finding the urge to sleep increasingly difficult to combat. At one point she dozed off on the sofa and only woke up when Milly placed her black and pink nose up against Jane's nose. Jane got up, disturbed by a momentary but frightening dream that she couldn't remember. She tried pacing around the house, but soon got bored and tired, and sat back down on the sofa. She spun round when she thought she heard someone behind her whispering her name. She tried to console herself that it was just an auditory hallucination. She readjusted the blanket that was covering the window so as not to see the shadows crowding in the dusky wood. Then she was dozing off again, and Milly was meowing. The ringing started in her head, and she was dozing off, and Milly was pawing at her leg. But she was too exhausted to react, and Milly was yowling, and her limbs were too heavy to lift, and she was falling asleep. Then she was in the woods.

Jane was wide awake, shivering with cold. It took her a moment to realise where she was, and then her fear nearly drove her out of her wits. She was in almost pitch blackness, the dry trees around her creaking and rattling despite the absence of wind. For a moment she had no idea which way to go, but then in the distance she saw the dim lights of Ash Wood Cottage. She took a tentative step in their direction, and then she heard someone whisper her name. Jane froze, but didn't turn around.

"Jane." The whisper came again – this time from a different direction. "Jane." Then another and another – encircling her – as though the wood itself were whispering her name from under every bush and behind every tree. Jane was sure now that she was losing her mind. Despite the dark and the uneven terrain, she tried to run, but from all around her came the sound that she had grown to dread. Her ears rang from the horrendous humming, which became a chanting – frightening, lulling, overpowering, mesmerising, rising in pitch and volume until it became like the scream of a million damned souls in hell, and coupling with the infernal drone of a boundless darkness that was reaching for her.

Visions of a terrifying nature swam before Jane – glimpses of things that no mortal should ever see. Shadowy, silhouetted figures swaying around a fire – some human, but others... others were horned, winged, animal-headed – ancient, horrifying creatures that had no right to walk among men. As the flames of the fire grew, the vision shifted, metamorphosed into a huge fiery pit in which burning souls screamed in perpetuity. And behind the torture and the carnage Jane could sense the hideous pulsing of the eternal abyss.

The sound in her head was unbearable. Jane was losing all sense of where she was, of who she was. The rhythmic pounding of the chanting and the fathomless darkness of the infinite void were all she could see and hear. A preternatural wind whipped up around her, trapping her in its vortex. Then the ice-cold tentacle was entering her head, her mind; probing like a violator inside her skull, her thoughts; its chill spreading through her very core. She battled it with all of her being. She tried to remember where she was, who she was – *I am Jane!* – but all she could feel was the numbing cold creeping inside her skull, exploring, expanding. *I am Jane.* All she could hear was the terrible din of the chanting and the sombre pulsating of the dark eons engulfing her. *I am...* And she was forgetting where she was and who she was, and the thing in her head was pushing and pushing. *I...*

And all that was left was a silent scream, and Jane was out of her body, and the wind was scattering her, and she was in the leaves, in the parched earth, in the gnarled blackened roots of the dark wood. She was festering in the dust and the dirt, and bugs were crawling over her and burrowing through her. She was in every rotted leaf and every dry twig and every wizened branch and every parched bit of dust, and small crawling things were devouring her and dying in her and rotting inside her. And she had no body, yet she could feel the things crawling and burrowing and eating and dying and rotting. She was nowhere. She was everywhere. On the ground, in the ground, in the putrefaction.

~

Monday 1st May (May Day)

She lay unconscious for hours on the forest floor. When her body finally twitched into life, she opened her eyes to the dawning of a fine May morning. She sat up slowly, looked at her unfamiliar hands, her feet, her legs, her body.

She was cold and streaked with dirt, but otherwise unharmed. She smiled as she got up calmly and started to make her way through the woods towards the cottage. As she crossed the fallen wire fence, she spotted Milly waiting on the lawn.

As she approached, the cat's fur bristled, tail several times its normal size, ears laid flat against her head in fear. Milly hissed and started backing away.

"You dare hiss at me?" she demanded of the petrified feline. "You will come here, like a good cat."

Milly dropped to her haunches and, quaking from nose to tail, crawled on her belly towards the cat sitter.

Isabelle and Jonathan got home tired. They'd left their car in one of Gatwick's long-stay car parks, and the drive from the airport wasn't particularly lengthy or strenuous, but the flight had been an early morning one and they hadn't had much sleep. By the time they walked through the front door it was gone midday.

"Hello!" Isabelle called out, setting down her suitcase at the bottom of the stairs. "We're home! Jane? Milly!" But the house was silent, and neither Jane nor Milly, who usually greeted her mistress with a castigating meow, were anywhere to be seen. "Milly! Here, Milly!"

Jonathan set the rest of the luggage down next to Isabelle's suitcase, and followed his wife into the sitting-room. The sight that greeted them stopped them in their tracks. Jane was sitting in Jonathan's favourite armchair, stroking Milly. The cat sat calmly and quietly on Jane's lap. Milly was a friendly cat, but she was no lap cat, and would meow loudly and wriggle free if ever Isabelle or Jonathan tried to hold her for any length of time or sit her on their laps.

"Wow!" Isabelle smiled at her friend in amazement, quickly dismissing the little stab of jealousy she suddenly felt over her cat's affections. "Look at the two of you! Best of friends!"

The creature that wore Jane's body smiled coldly back at Isabelle.

"Hello, Isabelle," she said. Her smile broadened visibly, transforming into a look that could only be described as lascivious as she turned her attention to Isabelle's husband. "Hello, Jonathan."

"Hi, Jane," Jonathan replied, a little puzzled, but not in a bad way. Jane usually looked at her feet when Jonathan addressed her – something he put down to her shyness and awkwardness around men. Isabelle threw her husband a disapproving look and he shrugged back.

"So, was everything okay when we were away?" Isabelle asked.

"Why wouldn't it be?" responded Jane, never taking her eyes off Jonathan. Isabelle studied her friend's leering face. Jane looked different somehow. She was wearing make-up. That was it: not only was she wearing make-up, but the shade of lipstick she'd applied thickly to her lips was identical to Isabelle's. Jane had been using Isabelle's make-up. Not just that, but she'd somehow squeezed into Isabelle's low-cut blue top and her short, stretchy black skirt.

"Uh, you're wearing my clothes," Isabelle finally said. Jonathan, who wasn't very observant when it came to ladies' fashion, looked at Isabelle in surprise, then back to Jane. There was indeed something familiar about the clothes that Jane was wearing, but they looked totally different on the larger girl, who was spilling out of them in a rather alluring way.

Jonathan was nonplussed to find himself feeling rather aroused. Jane finally turned her attention back to Isabelle.

"Oh yeah," she said. "I ran out of clean clothes and I didn't know how to use the washing-machine. I'll give them back before I leave."

"No problem," said Isabelle. But she wasn't buying the washing-machine story. Jane might be shy and frumpy and awkward, she might even sometimes give the impression of being a little slow, but she was sharp as anything when it came to figuring out how things worked. It was no coincidence that she'd been selected by her tutor at Oxford as the only girl to be part of the exchange with the American university. So no, Isabelle wasn't buying the washing-machine story, but she would let it slide. "You hungry, Jane?" she asked.

"Sure," Jane replied, all the while continuing to stroke Milly impassively. Milly didn't so much as twitch a muscle. She seemed completely mesmerised, her eyes staring into space like different coloured marbles. But she wasn't purring. And Isabelle suddenly had the bizarre notion that the cat was terrified into utter submission. She dismissed the idea immediately. She was tired, and seeing Jane all dolled-up like that, and in her clothes as well, had caught her off guard, but there was no need to start freaking out.

"Well, why don't you just relax," said Isabelle, heading out of the sitting room. "I'll have a quick shower and then I'll sort us out some lunch."

"Sure."

Isabelle paused in the doorway when she realised her husband wasn't following her.

"Honey?" She stared pointedly at her husband.

"What?" Jonathan tore his eyes away from Jane. "Oh, okay. I'm coming."

Jonathan reluctantly followed his wife upstairs and half-heartedly unpacked his suitcase while she showered.

"I doubt there's any food left," said Isabelle, rubbing her hair with a towel as she entered their bedroom. "What do you want to do?"

"I'm shattered, baby," said Jonathan. "I can't face getting back in the car. You wouldn't be able to pick up a few things while I shower and make a quick work call, would you?" There was a pause as Isabelle contemplated her husband's suggestion. A nasty paranoid thought about

Jane and Jonathan reared its ugly head in Isabelle's mind, but she dismissed it before it could fully form and take root. How could she even think such a thing for a moment? Jonathan had been nothing but loving and loyal to her ever since they met, and she hated herself for thinking ill of him even for a second.

"Sure, hon," she finally replied. "I'll be back soon."

Isabelle carefully backed the Land Rover out onto the road and headed for the village. She couldn't fathom what had happened to Jane. Jealousy – that was it. Isabelle had a home, a husband, a career, even a pet. Poor Jane had nothing. It was obvious that Jane's envy of everything that Isabelle had, and she didn't, had got the better of her. She'd somehow won over Milly by feeding her treats and spoiling her, and she'd thought she'd make a play for Jonathan too. Well, that was too much. Isabelle was sorry for her, but she was going to make damn sure that Jane never set foot in Ash Wood Cottage again. From now on, they'd use a local cat sitter.

Isabelle picked up four salmon fillets and some fresh fruit and veg from the village supermarket. By the time she was on her way home again, her anger had subsided and she even felt a little guilty about how glad she'd be to see the back of Jane. After all, Jane had come a long way and given up her bank holiday weekend to look after Milly. By the time she turned into the driveway, Isabelle had almost forgiven Jane. And then she felt even guiltier when she saw that Jane's car was gone. She walked into the kitchen and put down the groceries.

"Hello! Anybody home?" But there was no reply.

~

Friday 1ˢᵗ September

The paint had already started to flake on the FOR SALE sign outside Ash Wood Cottage. Had Isabelle decided to stay following Jonathan and Milly's disappearance, she might have noticed the change in the wood behind her house.

The trees were verdant, their leaves a lush and vibrant green in spite of autumn's rapid approach. Some of them still flowered despite the time of year, and sunlight streamed in through their mighty boughs. If a walker were to find themselves among the beauty of this ancient place, he or she might wonder at the moistness of the earth following such a dry summer. The ground was damp, muddy almost, as water seeped from the soil like tears.

Animals had moved into Ash Wood; from the undergrowth to the crowns of the tallest trees, the wood teemed with life. And yet for all its beauty, anyone who wandered into the wood emerged feeling pensive and somewhat sad. Even the birds that thrived in this quiet place sang a melancholy song.

Schrödinger's Human

The cat had the uncanny ability of seeming to be in two places at once, and it appeared logical to the man that he should name it Schrödinger. The cat evidently approved the name, purring as the man tried it out.

"Well, Schrödinger, I expect you *must* want some dinner *today*?" the man asked, backing away from the plate of cat food to allow the animal a chance to feed. But the cat stayed where it was, high up on the kitchen cupboard, and refused to give the cat food the time of day, just as it had refused milk and water, and even ham.

~

The man had first come across the cat on his return from work the previous day. It was thin and dirty, a mud-smeared black, with cold green eyes and a tattered left ear. The pitiful-looking thing was stretched out on his doorstep and refused to budge, even as the man approached. Instead it fixed him with an expectant stare and weaved its tail from side to side. The man studied the cat, and a long-forgotten joy stirred within him.

~

Ever since he was a child, the man had enjoyed torturing animals. His grandfather had bought him a butterfly net, and the boy quickly worked out that if you rubbed too much of the colourful dust off a butterfly's wings, it had trouble flying. And things got even more interesting if you pulled off its wings altogether and put it on an anthill. You could watch the black specks of the ants swarm all over the wounded intruder; watch the butterfly that was no longer a butterfly but a fascinating broken thing, try to lift itself out of the writhing mass of small stinging creatures, helplessly flailing its long thin legs, its proboscis furling and unfurling in some strange insect rhythm of pain.

Butterflies continued to fascinate for a long time, but eventually the allure of real animals –

ones which screamed and bled – took over from those that merely twitched pathetically. After much begging and family debate, he was finally given an air rifle for his birthday, but sadly this was confiscated when he moved up from shooting crows and squirrels to shooting the neighbours' pets. If necessity is the mother of invention, then a twisted imagination is its father, aunt and uncle. The boy came to understand that the air rifle which he had so mourned wasn't even a drop in the endless ocean of possibilities when it came to inflicting suffering on anything small and fluffy that had a heartbeat. And the smaller and fluffier it was, the easier it could be lured with a warm tone of voice, a friendly smile, a tickle behind the ear or, if all else failed, a piece of ham.

The boy tried a variety of techniques on his victims: dismemberment, disembowelment, decapitation, throwing off the roof or out of a window, the breaking of individual bones with a blunt instrument, blood-letting, crucifixion, and even electrocution – he was particularly good at this, as he had an excellent science teacher at school and displayed a definite propensity for the subject. But his favourite was luring a cat with the promise of food or affection, locking it in a cage and carrying it to his parents' roof, where he would douse its tail with petrol and set it alight before pushing it headfirst down the drainpipe. The trapped animal, its tail ablaze, would scream all the way down the drainpipe until it got stuck in a bend, where it would burn to charred bones and then fall out the bottom. This method only worked on small cats and kittens, but could also be applied to some breeds of puppy. The boy's attempts to involve the little girl next door in his pastime resulted in his being sent to a boarding school run by monks, where his sadistic horizons expanded to the use of canes, whips and rulers.

The boy left school with top results in science and went on to university, where his interest in animals waned somewhat, as his physics studies and unreciprocated fascination with girls led him to attain a First Class degree, despite almost being sent down for peeping through a female student's bedroom window. He stayed on in academia, eventually becoming a lecturer at a reputable university, where he could continue to indulge in physics and his unreciprocated fascination with girls.

And now here he was, trying to get home after a tiring day of lectures, and this scruffy, ugly cat was lying on his doorstep, as if daring him to gouge out its eyes and cut off its paws. Old passions awoke within the man, but he was too tired to act on them. He picked up a piece of brick that was lying in the roadside and aimed it between the cat's eyes. Just then a piercing pain shot through the man's temple. He dropped the brick and put his hands up to his head. As quickly as it had come, the pain was gone, but the man was left feeling bewildered and a little dizzy. As he rubbed his eyes to clear his head, he heard a voice close by his ear.

"Let me in," it said.

The man spun round, but there was nobody nearby – only the cat sprawled on his doorstep, eyeing him like a scientist eyes a mildly interesting specimen before dissection.

"Let me in," the voice continued, "and I'll show you things you've never seen... I'll take you to places you can't begin to imagine."

The man closed his eyes for a moment. When he opened them, the voice was gone and he felt his normal self again. He looked at his front door; the cat was no longer reclining, but sat alertly a couple of feet away from the door, as if waiting for the man to open it.

"What the hell," thought the man. If the cat wanted to come in, then let it. He was tired now, but he would amuse himself with the animal later. He opened the door and stood back to let the cat in. It eyed him suspiciously for a moment, then darted past, leaping over the threshold and heading straight for the kitchen.

The man followed it, locking the door behind him. He put his briefcase down in the hallway and went to see what the cat was doing. The kitchen was bathed in darkness and before the man switched on the light, he caught sight of the cat's eyes glowing in the shadows by the sink. But as the light from the overhead lamp illuminated the room, the man saw that the cat was not by the sink. Surprised, he looked around and spotted the creature sitting high on a kitchen cupboard, peering down at him with some curiosity and possibly a hint of malevolence.

"Well I'll be damned," he told the cat. "The rough and tumble world of quantum physics would have a field day with you." The man laughed at his own wit and went to the fridge to get some milk. If he was to get any use out of the cat, he'd have to start by getting it down from the kitchen cupboard.

But no end of coaxing would bring the cat down from its vantage point – not even a slice of premium ham. The man contemplated standing on a chair and dislodging the cat or throwing something at it, but he really couldn't be bothered. Besides, it would be much more fun to get the cat to trust him and then see the surprise in its furry little face when he took his penknife to it. The man made his own dinner, ate it and went through to the sitting-room to mark first-year physics assignments, leaving a plate of ham out to see if the cat would come down in his absence.

~

That night the man dreamt that he was walking through an unfamiliar landscape of red and black. The landscape was constantly shifting and changing. One moment he was walking along a mountain path, looking down into a valley of houses and fields, next he was in a labyrinth of tunnels, the walls made of human bones and skulls arranged in intricate patterns, one on top of the other. Somewhere ahead of the man a fire burned, and light from it bounced around the bone walls, bathing them in a warm glow and sending shadows flitting around the man. Beside him walked Schrödinger the cat, watching him with a modicum of curiosity, as if all this was familiar to the animal and it was merely interested in what the man made of it all – interested, but not *that* interested.

As the man approached the source of the flames, he became aware of the crackling sound they made. The crackling became a scratching, and the scratching grew louder until the man awoke. The scratching continued and the man realised that it was coming from his wardrobe. The damned cat had somehow gotten into it and was probably ruining his suits. He reached over to switch on his bedside lamp and recoiled as his fingers touched fur. The man sat upright and the cat leapt off the bedside table on which it had been sitting.

"Goddamn you, Schrödinger!" The man switched on the lamp and glared at the creature now sitting in the doorway. He swung his legs out of bed, but the cat had already gone. The man closed his bedroom door and went back to sleep.

~

In the morning the cat was back on the kitchen cupboard, and the ham was untouched on the plate where the man had left it the night before. The creature obviously hadn't eaten for a while and it had to be hungry. Either it was sick or it had been trained not to eat anything other than cat food. The man determined to buy some *Whiskas* on his way home from work.

But the cat wouldn't eat *Whiskas* or *Sheba* or *Felix*. It wouldn't drink milk or water and it wouldn't eat cat biscuits. In fact, it was a miracle that it was still alive. It was growing more emaciated by the day, and its protruding ribs only served to make it look scruffier and uglier. For a moment the man astonished himself by contemplating taking it to a vet, but quickly shrugged off such an insane idea and decided to kill it. He placed a kitchen chair next to the cupboard on which Schrödinger was perched, and went to get the meat cleaver. Then the doorbell rang.

The man put down the cleaver and went to answer the door. It was the teenage girl from the house next door.

"I'm sorry to bother you," she said, "but I'm locked out of the house. I forgot to take my keys this morning and my mum isn't back till seven. A couple of workmen followed me home from the high street and I don't want to wait outside. Can I hang out at yours until my mum gets back?"

The man studied the girl's short skirt and the way her blonde hair was pulled back in a ponytail, revealing the curve where her neck met her shoulder.

"Sure," he told the girl and stood aside to let her in. He cast a quick glance around the street. Sure enough, he saw two workmen loitering across the road, but they quickly turned on their heels and disappeared. There was no one else around.

"Would you like a cup of tea?" the man asked, leading the way to the kitchen.

"No thanks. Have you got any coke?"

"Yes." The man got a coke from the fridge and handed it to the girl. "Would you like a glass?"

"No thanks." The man indicated for the girl to

take a seat. That was when they both saw Schrödinger. It was standing on the kitchen table, tail twitching, staring at the girl.

"Oh, what a cute kitty!" cried the girl and moved towards the animal.

"Schrödinger, what the hell are you doing?" The tone in the man's voice stopped the girl in her tracks. The man moved forward, ready to swipe the cat off the table, but as he did so, the sharp pain in his head came, then went, and a voice near his ear said, "Kill her!"

"What?" exclaimed the man.

"What?" asked the girl, staring at the man uncomprehendingly.

"Nothing, honey, nothing."

But the voice came again, more persistent this time: "Kill her... now!"

The man felt confused. He looked at the girl. Her tanned arms and legs looked so inviting. A small artery in her neck was throbbing. The man found himself wondering how far the blood from that artery would spurt and whether it would reach the ceiling or just spatter the walls. He wondered whether the look of surprise in her eyes would be like that of the kittens and puppies he had dispatched to kitten and puppy heaven as a boy. He suspected that it would be better – much better – than anything he had experienced before. His cock was throbbing and he realised that the cat was staring at him, green eyes blazing, its customary disdain replaced by a feral excitement.

The artery in the girl's neck was still throbbing. Her lips were cherry red and a look of alarm was creeping over her face. She raised her hand to cover her mouth and, as she did so, her top rode up a little and the man could see the silver ring in her pierced belly-button. As time seemed to stop then stretch around the man, he noticed that the blue of the small gemstone on the ring matched the colour of the girl's eyes.

The artery in the girl's neck was throbbing, the man's cock was throbbing, and now a blood vessel in his head started to throb. The light in the kitchen seemed to throb and then the whole world was throbbing – a glorious red throbbing, pulsating, pounding. Then the meat cleaver was in the man's hand and the look of surprise in the girl's eyes was better than the puppies and the kittens – it was better than anything the man had experienced before, and the girl's blood was on the walls and on the ceiling and on the floor.

~

When the throbbing subsided, the man was sitting on the floor, his hands and clothes covered in blood. He felt calm and he felt good. The cat was standing beside him, face and whiskers stained red, frenziedly lapping up the girl's blood from the floor. The man stared at the animal in disbelief, but made no move to stop it. Despite the blood on its snout, the cat seemed less dirty than before: its fur seemed sleeker, it seemed somehow fatter and healthier, even its tattered ear seemed to have grown back together.

"Goddamn you, Schrödinger," the man said quietly, but the cat didn't even acknowledge his presence. It had cleaned the vast amount of blood off the floor and was now licking the girl's fingers. The man crawled around the girl's body to the hand that wasn't being worked on by the cat. He lifted the hand and sucked the blood from the index finger. It had a sickly taste, sweet and metallic. The man sucked on the girl's thumb and found that the taste was no longer sickly; it was, in fact, rather good.

A feeling of contented tiredness overcame

the man, and he dozed off right there, on the kitchen floor, next to the girl's lacerated body. When he woke up it was dark, and Schrödinger was nowhere to be seen. The man chopped up the girl's body with the meat cleaver, removing clothes, hair, bones and anything else that was inedible – this he would take to the municipal dump on his way to work tomorrow, along with the girl's faceless head. Everything else he washed and divided between his fridge and the freezer. He cleaned the walls as best he could, then dragged the kitchen table across and made an attempt to clean the ceiling. He would have to buy a large tin of paint and cover the stains that wouldn't wash off.

~

That night the man dreamt that he was standing over a precipice, looking down into a vast pit. The pit was filled with fire. The man noticed movement in the flames and realised that the pit was full of people – thousands of people – burning. He found that if he concentrated, he could hone in on individuals. He could clearly see the expressions of torment on their faces, the pain in their eyes. Their bodies were writing and their limbs flailing about helplessly. The man remembered the wingless butterflies flailing around on the anthill in his parents' garden, and smiled. He looked down and saw Schrödinger gazing up at him, reflections of the flames dancing in the animal's eyes.

~

Next morning the man awoke to purring by the side of his bed, but wasn't all that surprised to find that Schrödinger was not by his bed at all, but was waiting expectantly in the kitchen, sitting by the spot where the man had previously left its unwanted plate of cat food.

"Oh, so now you want to eat?"

The man knew what the cat wanted, but decided to tease it and put out a bowl of milk. But the joke was on him, as Schrödinger gave him such a look of malevolent contempt that the man's blood seemed to freeze in his veins and a nasty shiver went down his spine.

"Sorry," he said, and poured the milk down the sink. He got out a mincing machine and took some of the girl's flesh out of the fridge. He pushed it into the mincer and watched the pink worms come out the bottom. A sharp meow distracted him, and he glanced down to see Schrödinger dancing around on its hind paws, teeth bared. He put the mince on a clean plate, and hardly had time to place the plate on the floor before Schrödinger was upon it, wolfing down the meat like it hadn't eaten in days – which, after all, it hadn't. The man couldn't help thinking that if he hadn't withdrawn his hand in time, the animal might have devoured that too.

As he watched the cat feed, the man noticed how healthy it was looking. He thought he might have imagined it last night, in all the excitement, but in the cold light of day he could see that the cat's fur was a sleek, clean, shiny black, its protruding ribs had disappeared – concealed by a respectable plumpness – and its left ear looked like it had never encountered the Mike Tyson of the feline world.

The man cut a few thin slices of meat, and treated himself to a full English breakfast.

~

Over the next couple of weeks the cat and the man ate what was left of the teenager. The police came round and asked questions, but only the two workmen had seen the girl enter the man's house, and the police knew nothing of their existence. Officer Jones commented on the man's cute cat and Schrödinger purred obligingly, and that was that. Or would have been, except that the man couldn't stop thinking about the girl. Sometimes he worried about getting found out, but mostly he reminisced about the unbearably sweet sensation of plunging the meat cleaver into her soft flesh. His craving for more flesh and more blood wouldn't let him rest or concentrate on his work. Despite their shared diet, as the cat got fatter and silkier, the man lost weight, grew pale and haggard. When he slept, he dreamt of the burning pit and the bodies in it, writhing in perpetual torment. But mostly he just tossed and turned, listened to Schrödinger scratching in the wardrobe and watched its eyes glow by the side of his bed.

About the time that the girl meat ran out, the man's cravings reached an unbearable pitch. He was horny and hungry and confused all at the same time. He was distracted in his tutorials and it was just a matter of time before one of the students complained. Schrödinger was refusing to eat anything that wasn't human, and its body was atrophying. Its left ear was hanging in tatters by the side of its head, and its teeth started falling out, so that its tongue protruded, giving it a rather unsavoury and slightly demented expression. It eyed the man with barely disguised contempt, and the man found himself feeling increasingly uncomfortable around it.

~

The student was only in her first term, but she was already behind in her work. She had been good at physics at school, but university was different. The professor was bombarding them with new information every day, and they were expected to come up with their own ideas and solutions to problems. When the professor asked to see her, she was terrified that she was in trouble. She was relieved when he spoke kindly to her and offered to spend some time with her, going over problems they had tackled in class, to help her catch up with the others. The professor explained that he had a variety of textbooks at home and it would be easier if she dropped by his house, where they would have all the books at hand.

"I realise that young ladies sometimes feel uncomfortable being alone with a man," he told her, "and you are very welcome to bring a friend with you, as long as your friend won't mind keeping my cat company while we're studying."

"You have a cat?" the girl smiled.

"His name's Schrödinger. He's very friendly and he's especially fond of young ladies."

The girl smiled again and lowered her eyes.

"Do you have a friend you would like to bring?"

The man knew full well that the girl had no friends. Shy and from a state school, unlike the privileged majority of the students, he often saw her sitting alone in the lecture hall and leaving alone when the lectures were over.

"Oh, that's okay," the girl replied. "I don't feel uncomfortable."

"Well, that's just fine. My cat would love to meet you. He's been feeling a little under the weather lately."

~

The plan seemed fool proof, but when the student arrived at his house, the man found himself having second thoughts. This was not something he'd envisaged – he'd wanted another girl desperately for weeks. But when he saw her standing on his doorstep in her knee high socks and pink sweater, physics notes in a file under her arm, his palms suddenly felt clammy and a nerve under his eye started to twitch. She was his student, after all, and maybe that meant that he was crossing some kind of line – a line between fair game and... well... not.

"Come in," he told the girl, seriously considering actually giving her a physics lesson. But as soon as he shut the door behind her and ushered her into the kitchen, Schrödinger was there in front of them, meowing and twitching its tail.

"Oh," exclaimed the girl, "he doesn't look too well."

"He hasn't been eating properly," the man explained. "In fact, he's been feeling rather sorry for himself, but I'm sure he'll cheer up now that you're here."

The girl stooped down to stroke the cat, but something in its unappetising appearance and intent stare put her off. She straightened up and smiled at the professor, who offered her a cup of tea and put the kettle on.

The cat meowed loudly and the man tried to swipe at it behind the girl's back. But the pain in his head was back. The man winced and clapped his hands to his temples.

"Are you okay, professor?" There was concern in the girl's brown eyes.

But the pain in his head was gone, and the dizzy feeling was back, and the voice was telling him to kill.

"Professor? Are you feeling alright?"

But the kettle was in his hand and, before he knew it, he was pouring boiling water over the girl's face and she was too shocked to make a sound as her face started to blister. And then he was bashing the girl over the head with the kettle, bashing her face and bashing her chest and bashing the base of her skull. The girl slid to the floor, but still he kept hitting her. He could feel his skin burning as some of the boiling liquid splashed on his hands, but still he kept smashing the girl with the kettle until her head was a bloody pulp and her legs ceased twitching. Then he stopped. He put the kettle down and went to the sink, soaking his hands under the cold water tap until he was fairly confident that they wouldn't blister. He glanced occasionally over his shoulder at the cat, which was greedily lapping up the puddle of blood beneath the dead girl's head.

The cleaning and carving took a long time and the man went to bed exhausted. He fell asleep quickly and dreamt that he was falling into the burning pit. He fell slowly, and had ample opportunity to watch and feel the flames getting closer. The rising heat overtook him on his way down and, by the time he reached the bottom of the pit, his flesh was already blistering and smoking. His skin caught fire and was burnt away, and, as the flames reached the fat beneath, the man went up like a torch. He tried to scream, but his throat was burning on the inside. He looked up and saw Schrödinger looking down at him from the edge of the pit. The cat's expression was one of mild amusement.

~

The following day the man determined to kill Schrödinger. He minced some meat, laid it out on a clean plate and put it down in front of the waiting cat. While the creature was preoccupied, the man opened the drawer and took hold of the meat cleaver. The pain hit his head like a spear and he dropped the cleaver back in the drawer. He looked over at Schrödinger, but the cat didn't even interrupt its meal long enough to cast him an evil glance.

~

It was a while before anyone reported the student missing. The police came to the campus and interviewed everyone who knew her. The interviews didn't last long, as even those students who recognised her picture weren't able to provide any information about the girl. But Officer Jones recognised the physics professor as the next door neighbour he had interviewed in his previous unsolved missing girl case, and decided to pay him a home visit, complete with warrant.

~

Officer Jones arrived at the house with two other policemen. If the man was shocked to see three police officers on his doorstep, he didn't show it. He invited them in politely and stood back as they ransacked his home.

Officer Jones spotted a pair of green eyes in the shadows under the coffee table in the sitting-room, and remembered the man's cat. He had a soft spot for cats and bent down to the animal, but saw to his surprise that the space under the coffee table was empty. As he straightened up, he noticed the cat sitting on an armchair at the far side of the room, watching him. Before he had a chance to approach the animal, one of the other officers summoned him from the bedroom. He hurried over to his colleague.

Officer Trevayne was standing by the open drawer of the man's bedside cabinet, holding a silver belly-button ring with a small blue gemstone in his latex-gloved hand. Officer Jones recognised it immediately from a photograph given to him by the parents of the missing girl from the house next door. He moved rapidly out into the hallway, where Officer Green was waiting with the man.

"Sir, we need you to come with us to the station, to answer some questions," Officer Jones told the man. For the briefest moment the man looked shaken, but regained his composure almost instantly.

"Of course," he said. "Anything I can do to

help... I'll just grab my coat." The man went over to the coat stand and reached for his coat, but just then he felt the familiar stabbing pain in his head. It came and went, leaving him confused as to how it was that he'd lifted the heavy coat stand and why it was that he brought the full weight of it down on Officer Green – brought the large wooden object down again and again on the policeman, until he felt a stinging pain rip through his shoulder, and the whole world went red, then black.

~

Officer Jones put his gun away and radioed for an ambulance. He moved swiftly over to the man and checked his pulse; the bullet had passed straight through his heart and the man was dead within seconds. It was a bad situation, but the man would have killed Officer Green – if he hadn't already done so. Officer Jones knelt beside Officer Trevayne, who was tending to their badly wounded colleague.

"He's alive," said Officer Trevayne, "but he needs to get to a hospital ASAP."

"I'll go outside and flag the ambulance down."

But as Officer Jones moved towards the front door, he felt a sharp pain in his temple. He winced and put his hand up to his head, but the pain was gone, replaced by a slight feeling of nausea and bewilderment. This in turned passed, and a voice spoke in the policeman's ear.

"Take me with you," it said. "I'll show you things you've never seen."

Officer Jones looked round and saw the black cat eyeing him dispassionately.

The train journey was exhausting. The removal company was going to deliver most of their things, but even the basics that Emily's mother had insisted they take themselves filled three heavy suitcases, a hold-all and several ungainly plastic bags. Miraculously they had managed to load everything onto the train before it departed, but Emily couldn't stop worrying about how they would get it all off at the other end. She dozed off during the long ride, but her sleep was fitful, her anxiety giving rise to a horrible dream. Not only were they unable to get all the luggage off on time, but her mother disappeared and the train left with Emily and her pet still on it, taking them to a dark, deserted place, where she got separated from Bagpuss and didn't know how to get home. From this she awoke sweating and headachy.

"What is it, dear?" asked her mother, in that tired, indifferent tone that had been in her voice ever since Emily's father had walked out one day and never come back.

"Nothing," said Emily, relieved that it had been just a dream. Her worries still played on her mind though. She moved the cat carrier slightly and peered in through the bars at Bagpuss, who meowed – a plaintive, pathetic, frightened little noise, cute in a kitten perhaps, but strangely unnerving in a large, lazy, eight-year-old tabby lap-cat. Bagpuss had been emitting similar sounds ever since Emily and her mother had forced him into the blue cat carrier. He had struggled with all his might, wedging his paws against the plastic around the opening of the box and tensing up his entire body with strength extraordinary for a being a fraction of the size of the two humans trying to push him in. But as soon as the battle was lost and the bars of the cat carrier came down before his eyes, he started mewling in the tiny yet penetrating way of an unwanted kitten destined for a stone-laden sack at the bottom of a lake.

"It's okay," Emily told him, "I'm here. I won't let anything bad happen to you."

~

Bagpuss had been with Emily since he was six weeks old, but he had been silent as a kitten, and had only found his tongue at a later age, sparsely using a low, gruff meow to indicate that he was hungry or wanted to go outdoors. Mostly, he would lie on Emily's lap, purring loudly and sometimes even snoring. So the eerie little squeaks and cries were something new and distressing to his twelve-year-old mistress – as new and distressing as having to leave her city life and move to the countryside, away from her room, her house, her street, and everything that made her feel safe. New things, new places, new people had no appeal to her; they gave her a nasty tight sensation in the pit of her stomach – a feeling like something really bad was about to happen; a feeling that had increased in frequency since her father had left. Now that they were on the train and heading for her new home, the feeling of impending doom was stronger than ever, and Emily was convinced that Bagpuss felt it too.

~

"How many more stations before we get there?" Emily asked her mother.

"I don't know, dear."

"You have to ask someone, mummy."

"Why?"

"We have to get ready to get off the train before it reaches the station. Otherwise we won't have time to get everything off."

"Of course we will."

"But we have to get ready before we get to the station, mummy."

Emily's agitation was starting to break through the protective barrier of Valium and worry her mother. The child had always been timid and oversensitive, but lately she was stressing about everything. Emily's mother tried to remember being twelve. She had been brought up in the countryside and remembered her childhood as being full of sunny days – helping out on the farm, cycling with her friends, running down to the river to fish or remove socks and shoes and paddle – unstressed and carefree. Not like Emily, who always fretted about everything. And her father leaving had provided the perfect opportunity for the child's anxiety to run wild. Perhaps life in the country would be good for the girl. Perhaps a new start in life was what they both needed.

~

As they pulled into the village station, all their things were already by the train door – at Emily's insistence, of course – and Emily was firmly clutching Bagpuss's cat carrier to her chest.

"Mummy, I'll go first and put Bagpuss down, and then I'll help you get the suitcases down, but you'll have to pass them to me because I don't want to leave Bagpuss on his own on the platform because someone might steal him."

"Nobody's going to steal Bagpuss."

"Well, a dog might attack the cat carrier and Bagpuss might get hurt."

"Nothing's going to happen to Bagpuss," sighed Emily's mother.

"Yes, but you don't know that, mummy. I have to stay on the platform with him to make sure he doesn't think we've abandoned him and get scared."

"Very well, Emily. You stay on the platform with Bagpuss and I'll pass the bags down to you."

The unloading went smoothly, apart from Bagpuss's desperate mewling as his miniature prison got moved again and the cat temporarily lost the ground under his feet, his whole world shaking and lurching until Emily placed the carrier down on the platform – on solid ground now, but still imprisoned and claustrophobic.

There were no cabs at the station, but the station master phoned for one and, after a long wait, a man in his sixties arrived and somehow helped them load all their belongings into his battered old Ford. The man chatted away to Emily's mother and eyed her with an interest that made Emily nervous. The girl ignored the cab driver, and concentrated her attentions on Bagpuss, who had fallen deathly quiet in his sweaty prison.

"It's a ten-minute drive," her mother had told her, and five minutes into the journey the feeling of impending doom in Emily's stomach had grown to a level which made her want to clutch her abdomen. Instead, she hugged Bagpuss's cage tightly. The cat yelped, and Emily was certain that he was sharing her fear of what was to come.

Five minutes later, and the three of them –

Emily, Emily's mother and Bagpuss in his plastic cage – were standing in front of their new home. Emily's mother had turned down the cab driver's repeated offer of helping them carry their bags into the house, but had taken the business card on the back of which he had jotted his home phone number. And Emily finally understood the feeling in the pit of her stomach that she'd had since she was little – the feeling that crept over her in the middle of the day or in the dead of night; the feeling that grew as she tossed and turned in her bed – formless and indescribable until it took shape and found expression in her nightmares and anxiety dreams: those dreams of finding ourselves naked in front of others, of facing an examination paper without knowing the curriculum, of fleeing from something unspeakable along corridors that get narrower and narrower until we can scarcely breathe...

Emily trembled as she looked up at her new home, and knew that the recurrent feelings of impending doom had all led to this: the brooding dark house whose eaves cast a shadow that somehow managed to reach her and make her shiver on this fine summer afternoon. A house whose dark corners would devour her, and her mother and her cat. Even the roses climbing ramshackle up the walls of the house were the colour of congealed blood, their scent suffocating, their thorns waiting to scar anyone who came close. But worse still – worse than the house with its bloody roses and windows gaping like cataract-covered eyes – was the untamed expanse of land behind the house. A wilderness of plants, spiky and barbed, ready to impale anyone who ventured among them. Tangled roots ready to wind themselves around an ankle and bring its owner crashing into the spider-infested undergrowth. A place teeming with unseen life, a thousand creatures – scurrying, crawling, watching, waiting. And beyond all that: a dark tree line looming ominously on the horizon.

Emily felt faint. All she had ever known were the familiar streets of the city in which she had lived all her life – streets with names that made sense and instilled a feeling of security: First Avenue, Second Avenue, Third Avenue; streets that criss-crossed each other at reliable right-angles, forming orderly squares with houses and shops where they intersected. Even the parks were safe – the grass neatly mown, the trees arranged symmetrically, planted evenly apart, their branches trimmed regularly so that they could not grow into monstrous limbs which reached for you and tried to drag you into a scratching, deadly embrace... Velvety moss, scented wild herbs and colourful meadow flowers brought Emily no comfort. What should have been a Garden of Eden was to Emily a Garden of Evil.

Bagpuss mewed wildly in his cat carrier – no longer a tiny, pitiful squeal, but a feral, desperate cry – and threw himself against the bars, rattling the plastic cage so hard that Emily feared it would overturn and harm her pet. She carried the box with the wailing, thrashing animal up to the house and, once her mother unlocked the door, inside. Emily made sure the front door was securely closed again, put down the cage and opened it carefully. Bagpuss sprang out faster than Emily thought possible, and headed straight for the front door, scratching at it feverishly.

"You'd better let him out," Emily's mother told her. "I have to open the door in any case, to bring our bags in."

"But Mummy..."

"He'll be fine."

"Okay. But I'll go with him."

"Don't you want to have a look around the house?"

Emily cast a fearful glance past her mother, at the murky hallway with doors leading off it, and the winding staircase leading up into darkness.

"Maybe later," she told her mother and turned her attention back to her frantically meowing, scratching cat.

~

As soon as Emily opened the front door, Bagpuss bolted out like the proverbial bat out of hell and took off down the porch steps.

"Bagpuss, wait!"

The cat reached the bottom of the steps and paused, looking around, sniffing the air, droopy whiskers and fluffy tail twitching nervously. Bagpuss had never known a world such as this. His cruel imprisonment in the evil-smelling plastic cage was all but forgotten, as a universe of magnificent scents, sights and sounds burst open all around him. It was as though he had sleep-walked through his life and now, finally, he was wide awake – his nerves tingling with excitement and the blood singing in his veins.

Bagpuss hardly noticed as Emily caught up with him and spoke to him softly.

"There you are, Bagpuss." Emily reached down and stroked the cat gently. Bagpuss became aware of his friend next to him, and looked up at her, purring loudly. He could smell the lush scent of the roses clinging to the walls of the house behind him. He could smell wild flowers and herbs, birds, mice and other small creatures in the bushes all around. But Bagpuss could smell something else too – an alluring, intoxicating scent, and it was calling him. The cat quivered from the tip of his pink nose to the tip of his black and grey tail, then set off at a trot.

"Bagpuss, wait!" Emily ran after her pet, terrified of losing sight of him. She found him standing behind the house, gazing across the expanse of meadow towards the woods on the horizon. Bagpuss's nose twitched as he took in that wonderful scent – it was the fragrance of the warm grass before him, it was the scent of open space – the smell of freedom. He took off across the field.

"No, Bagpuss! You're going too far!" Emily

followed her cat, trying not to fall as the branches of strange plants curled around her ankles; increasingly distressed as she kept losing sight of the cat in the tall grass.

As Bagpuss bounded over the exotic landscape, the breeze ruffled his fur, and the sounds of birdsong and of small frightened creatures scurrying away through the grass caressed his ears. Even through all the new aromas of plants and animals, Bagpuss noticed another, stronger smell. He slowed down, years of dozing on Emily's sofa having taken their toll on his natural feline stamina, but continued to press ahead, until the strange new scent was joined by a rushing, gurgling sound. As he navigated the last few metres of grass between him and the noisy thing ahead, Emily cried out behind him.

"Oh my God! No, Bagpuss, no!"

But Bagpuss had already burst out onto the river bank, and was staring down at the river – narrow at this point, only a few metres across – silver and blue-grey, light dancing between the brown and dark green reflections of the trees that grew on its other side.

As the cat stared in awe at the flowing water,

the dancing light, he caught sight of movement made by something more solid – it was a fish. Bagpuss carefully made his way down to the water and contemplated sticking in a paw.

"Bagpuss, no!" In the second that it took Bagpuss to glance back at Emily, the fish was gone. Then Emily was picking him up, enveloping him gently in her arms, her scent familiar and soporific.

"You mustn't go near the river, it's not safe." Bagpuss was disappointed to be leaving the riverbank, but he was tired now, and after an initial half-hearted squirm, he allowed himself to be carried back to the house.

That night it took Emily a long time to get to sleep. The latter part of the day had passed uneventfully, apart from unpacking their suitcases and bags. The men from the removal company were not due until the following morning, and Emily's mother had brought enough food to do the three of them for dinner and for breakfast the following morning. Emily had nervously explored the house, and put away the few items of clothing that she had brought with her in the large old wardrobe of the room that her mother had chosen for her. The room was sombre enough during the day, but at night darkness lay thick in its nooks and crannies, and the tree outside sent restless shadows scuttling over Emily's window and scratched at the glass panes when the breeze stirred it. When the last light had faded from the sky, the darkness outside was profound – nothing like the polluted orange glow of city night. Emily pulled her blanket up to her chin and listened fearfully to the silence, broken only by Bagpuss snoring at the foot of her bed – but even the comforting sound of the sleeping cat did little to still Emily's racing heart.

When she finally fell asleep, Emily dreamt of the frightening expanse of land leading down to the river behind the house and the verdant darkness of the woods beyond. She was trying to keep sight of Bagpuss among the long grass and meadow flowers. It was magic hour, and the field around Emily glowed in the eerie, beautiful, alien light. The smell of the flowers and wild herbs was at its strongest, the sultry remains of the hot day enhancing the various scents, making them intoxicating, stifling.

"Bagpuss! Wait!" As Emily hurried in the direction where she had just seen the tip of

Bagpuss's tail disappear, she became aware that she was not alone out here with her cat. She slowed down, looking around nervously, and shrieked as a flash of dry lightning lit up the field and she spotted eyes in the grass, all around, watching her. Emily started to panic, glancing this way and that, and the hundreds of cornflowers stared back at her, their piercing cornflower eyes unnaturally blue in the strange light, staring at Emily suspiciously, accusingly, as if they knew something about her that she didn't know herself.

Emily trembled, then, seeing her cat leaping over a clump of dandelions some way ahead, she moved to head off after him, but stopped again as an ear-rending screech silenced the insects in the grass nearby. Emily looked around fearfully. The screech came again, and that was when she saw the poppy. The flower stared at Emily, then swayed from side to side on its stem until it seemed to haemorrhage into a cockerel with deep red plumage and a scarlet crest. As Emily watched, horrified, the thing continued to shake itself violently until its crest dripped blood, rending open its fear-poisoned beak and screaming at Emily until she turned and raced towards the river and the dark tree line beyond. As she ran, Emily noticed the single ears of wild barley growing here and there in the field. She tried to skirt around one, but skimmed it with her foot and stopped as the plant glistened with a golden hue. Emily stared as the plant bristled its husks angrily and, emitting a hollow rattling sound, ground itself into a golden hedgehog and ran from her, pricking the slender wild herbs that stood in its way.

Emily clapped her hands to her temples and headed for the river, a terrible fear for Bagpuss rising within her. As soon as it had come, magic hour was over, and the last of the light bled from the sky. As Emily reached the bank of the river she heard a loud splash and she cried out.

"Bagpuss! Bagpuss!" But there was no answer, no familiar meow, only a faint splash in the river some distance away. Emily stared into the inky depths of the river and finally she saw Bagpuss – a little way off, his paws flailing helplessly as he tried to stay afloat. As Emily jumped into the cold river, an undercurrent suddenly caught Bagpuss and pulled him under the dark water. Emily screamed and threw herself in the direction of her beloved pet. For a moment Bagpuss's head bobbed up above the water and Emily half-swam half-ran towards him, but the current got a hold of him and carried him away downstream. Tears streaming down her face, Emily swam after her cat.

Darkness had set in fast and Emily could hardly distinguish the black water from the blackness all around her. She could just make out Bagpuss ahead of her, tossed about by the current. With a huge effort she finally reached him and pulled him out of the water, clutching him to her, and managed to get him to the shore. Wet through, he was no longer big and fluffy, but small and vulnerable. She tried to warm his little body against her neck and shoulder, but he was stone cold and limp.

"Wake up, Bagpuss, wake up!" she begged, but it was too late. Emily cried and cried, and hugged Bagpuss's dead body until she woke up to find her pet very much alive, his nose pressed up against her face, eyeing her with a look of concern.

"Oh, Bagpuss," cried Emily and squeezed the surprised cat until he yelped and removed himself to the armchair in the corner of the room.

The next morning Bagpuss woke Emily bright and early, demanding to be let out. Emily refused to open the front door and clapped her hands over her ears, ignoring the cat's urgent meowing. It wasn't until Emily's mother found a pool of cat pee by the front door that Emily was reprimanded and, after much debate and tear-shedding, Bagpuss was allowed to explore the boundlessness of the land behind the house once more.

The men from the removal company arrived with the rest of the clothes, the furniture, kitchen utensils, Emily's prized collection of stones and pebbles – which Emily laid out according to size on the large windowsill in her bedroom – and the thing that Emily had been waiting for most: Bagpuss's cat litter. Emily hoped that Bagpuss would start relieving himself in the litter again, and wouldn't need to leave the house. But her hopes were dashed, as the cat spurned the litter entirely and spent all of the time that he was awake either outdoors or sitting by the front door, begging to be let out.

As time wore on, Emily found herself increasingly alone. Bagpuss no longer sat on her lap or played with the cloth mouse that she sometimes dragged around in front of him on a piece of string. He still slept in Emily's room, but he was coming home increasingly late and demanding to be let out increasingly early. During the day, Emily would try to follow Bagpuss, spending as much time outdoors – among the heady-scented flowers and crawling insects – as her mother would allow, trying to make sure that nothing happened to her cat. But when Emily's mother insisted on her doing chores, or accompanying her to the village grocery store, or doing some homework in preparation for the beginning of term in her new school once summer was over, Emily spent every moment worrying about Bagpuss. When her mother made her go to bed before Bagpuss had come home, Emily would lie awake, her mind conjuring up blood-curdling images of her beloved pet drowning, being torn apart by foxes, being decapitated by local juvenile delinquents fancying themselves as Satanists, being bitten by a rabid bat or getting stuck in a rabbit hole and starving to death. In those dark, lonely hours Emily imagined every horror possible – except...

~

The car was a brand new bottle green Land Rover driven by a twenty-four year-old banker. It was difficult to put the SUV through its paces in London – too many speed cameras – but the winding country lanes in this part of the world were just bliss. You could easily do the curves at 90 miles an hour, and the straight stretches of road... well... there was no limit – only the size of your balls.

~

The mouse was small and grey, and running for its life. Bagpuss could tell that it was tiring and he fancied his chances. All the time he had spent roaming the wilderness behind the house and chasing any critter that was smaller than him had paid off. His portliness had been replaced by a firm layer of muscle, and his senses were no longer dulled by hours of snoozing in front of the telly. He had yet to actually catch something, but today was going to be the day. He'd nail the damned mouse, but he wouldn't eat it himself; he would carry it up to Emily's room and place it on her bed to show her how much he loved her.

The mouse sprinted past the house, Bagpuss hot on its tail. Blind with fear, the mouse burst out onto the main road that led to the village, and the cat leapt after it. The impact with the metal grille threw Bagpuss into the air and he landed in the road, the Land Rover's shining silver alloy wheels directing the entire weight of the vehicle onto his small furry body. The SUV didn't even slow down. The mouse disappeared into the undergrowth on the far side of the road and, as dusk fell, a fox snatched up what was left of Bagpuss and carried it back to its hungry family.

~

Emily waited for Bagpuss to come home. She polished her stones and pebbles over and over, hardly aware of what she was doing. At midnight her mother caught her trying to sneak out of the house to look for her pet and sent her, wailing, up to bed. Emily spent most of the night peering out of her window into the darkness beyond, and eventually cried herself to sleep as the dawn chorus started up outside her window.

The days that followed were akin to a never-ending version of one of Emily's anxiety dreams.

She spent every free moment of daytime wandering around the wasteland at the back of the house, calling Bagpuss's name. At night, the silence was unbearable, the tree outside her window scratched the glass like nails on a chalkboard and the shadows in her room crowded around her menacingly. Ever since her father had left, Bagpuss had slept in Emily's room, his snoring making her giggle, but never keeping her awake for long. And as with the time after her father had first departed, Emily was in a permanent state of suspension – waiting rather than living – the anxious feeling in her stomach making her nauseous with dread.

As Emily's anxiety grew, she developed a fear of being alone – especially at night. One night, when a strong breeze animated the tree in a particularly alarming way, she turned up in her mother's room and asked if she could sleep with her.

"No," Emily's mother replied, her voice groggy with Valium-induced sleep. "You're far too old for that." Emily returned to her own room and cried the night away. At about midday she was woken by the sound of the phone ringing. She went downstairs and peered into the kitchen, where she could see her mother speaking on the telephone, her face disconcertingly lively – not at all like the tired, resigned face that Emily had grown accustomed to. Emily asked her mother who had called. "No one," her mother replied, looking embarrassed and quickly changing the subject. That day Emily didn't go out to look for Bagpuss, but followed her mother around the house, even offering to accompany her to the grocery store.

For the next few days, Emily went everywhere with her mother, and now sat watching tensely as her mother relaxed reading a Mills and Boon novel after finishing the housework. Eventually Emily's mother could stand her intent gaze no longer.

"Shouldn't you be out looking for Bagpuss?" she asked.

"He's not coming back," replied Emily morosely. "They never do."

"What's that supposed to mean?"

"Nothing." Emily dropped her gaze to the floor.

"Well, why don't you call those nice girls we met at the grocery store the other day – I'm sure they'd love to play with you."

"I'd rather stay here with you."

"Well, you're going to need to find something to occupy yourself with by the weekend. I'm going out on Saturday."

"What?" Emily looked like she'd been slapped in the face.

"I'm going out on Saturday... don't look so shocked. I have a right to a life, you know."

"Where are you going?"

"To a dance."

"Who with?"

"Les."

"Who's Les?" Emily was looking increasingly frightened.

"Les... The man who drove us here."

"The cab driver?"

"He drives a cab to earn a living, but he's really a writer."

Emily was trying hard to get a handle on what was happening. After a long pause, she asked: "Can I come?"

"No, Emily. You can't come."

"Fine," said Emily, and ran out of the room so that her mother wouldn't see the tears welling up in her eyes. Her mother was going to leave her. With the cab driver. First her father, then

Bagpuss, and now her mother. Emily would die here – in this big dark house – get sick and die all alone, and by the time they found her body it would be mauled by rats and covered in spiders, and flies would have laid their eggs in her and she would be crawling with maggots. She had to stop her mother leaving.

Emily put her coat on and headed out of the house.

"Where are you going?" Her mother came out of the sitting-room.

"I'm going to play with the kids we met at the grocery store."

"Oh." Her mother was surprised by this sudden U-turn. Then again, Emily was almost a teenager now, and her strange, unpredictable behaviour was probably just a symptom of her age.

~

It was getting late by the time Emily returned from the internet cafe, hiding a bunch of printouts behind her back as her mother questioned her about what she had been doing with the girls from the grocery store. Emily seemed calmer at dinner than she had been for a while, and her mother was pleased that her new friends were helping her to get over Bagpuss's disappearance.

But Emily was more anxious than ever, and that night she had the nightmare again. She was stumbling after Bagpuss through the meadow at the back of her house, the sky lit up by dry lightning, and the flowers and weeds mutating painfully into grotesque animals and birds that pecked and snapped at her heels, screeching wildly. The sky grew darker and, as Emily reached the river, she heard a splash and threw herself into the inky water, crying out her pet's name. But as Emily reached the spot where her cat had gone under the water for the last time, as she dived down and grabbed him, it was not Bagpuss she pulled out of the murky depths, it was the pale-faced corpse of her mother. Emily screamed and woke herself up. She got out of bed and crept to her mother's room, standing silently for long minutes and listening to her mother's regular breathing as she slept.

Emily was determined to go through with her plan. And she had to act fast as Saturday was only two days away. The poison was easy enough to buy, as many of the rural houses had problems with rats, and the local store stocked a variety of rodent-killing products. Emily's research provided her with all the information she needed to carry out her plan. The idea had first come to her when she remembered a murder mystery she had seen on television: a man had killed his wife over the period of a year by giving her small amounts of poison in her food – too small to kill her immediately, but enough to make his wife progressively more sick until eventually she died. Of course Emily did not want to kill her mother – quite the opposite. She wanted her mother to stay with her forever. She would never give her mother enough poison to make her really sick; just enough to make her feel a little poorly. Emily would look after her mother and tend to her every need, so that after a while her mother would not even want to go out; she would come to rely on Emily, to appreciate her and be grateful for her company. And she certainly would not want to leave with the cab driver.

That evening Emily's mother was in a strange mood. It would have been her fourteenth wedding anniversary if her husband hadn't left her. She couldn't for the life of her remember if she had taken her Valium or not. Emily was being neurotic again, following her around the house and trying to talk to her, but she was far too tired to cope with Emily's quirks today. When Emily surprised her by making her a cup of hot chocolate, she took the mug, but decided to drink it in bed.

Emily's mother placed the mug on her bedside table and went to the bathroom cabinet. Perhaps she hadn't taken her Valium after all. She took one out of the prescription bottle and, after a moment's hesitation, she took out another. She carried the pills through to her bedroom and, climbing into bed, washed them down with the hot chocolate. After a while she started to feel sick. She doubled up in pain and reached out for the bedside table to steady herself, knocking off the lamp, which smashed on the floor.

~

Emily heard the noise in her mother's room and rushed over. The sight that greeted her was more terrifying than any nightmare she had ever had. Her mother was thrashing around in the bed, blood and vomit all over her nightgown.

"Mummy!"

~

By the time the ambulance arrived, the suffering of Emily's mother was over. After pronouncing the woman dead, the paramedic looked around the house for the girl who had called in to say that her mother was very sick.

~

Emily headed across the wilderness, her movements slowed by the stones and pebbles that were stretching the pockets of her coat. She barely noticed the nettles that stung her ankles and the thistles that scratched her arms. Her eyes were fixed on the tree line beyond the river and she thought she could see the tip of Bagpuss's tail ahead of her in the darkness. As she reached the riverbank, there was a splash, and the inky water closed over her head as she fell forward and allowed the stones and the current to pull her down.

> "...thou art the Great Cat, the avenger of
> the gods, and the judge of words, and
> the president of the sovereign chiefs,
> and the governor of the holy Circle..."
> *From a tomb inscription in the Valley of the Kings*

It had been a hard but satisfying day. The girl had fought valiantly for her life – particularly given her slight build and tender age – and the very process of bagging up her body and weighing it down with stones before depositing it into just the right spot in the canal had been physically draining. The man took a sip of his pint and gazed absentmindedly at the cat with the unusual markings that had been his constant drinking companion ever since he'd started frequenting *The Organ Grinder*.

The cat's coat was the light sandy brown of the desert at dusk, with a cream throat and belly, narrow bands of dark fur around its legs and black-tipped tail, and rings of white fur around its eyes. The eyes themselves were the colour of sun-washed savannah, and long pale hairs sprouted on the insides of its delicately tufted orangey-brown ears. Its whiskers were long and white, its nose a salmon pink, and a dark stripe ran the length of its back.

The man's thoughts turned from the cat back to the day's events and he smiled to himself. He'd first chosen the girl – or 'marked her' as he liked to think of it – a month earlier. After that it was simply a matter of following her home, observing her movements, working out her daily routine, and picking the best time and place to make his move.

As the time approached, the waiting, the watching, the anticipation had become almost unbearable, but in the end worth every minute – as it always was. The profound sense of calm he now felt would last for a couple of weeks – perhaps more, given the souvenir that he'd kept: a heart-shaped locket containing a photo of the smiling faces of the girl and her best friend. He'd keep the little silver-plated pendant in his secret place, and could take it out whenever he wanted to relive the day's events. When the burning need took a hold of him again, the whole process would begin anew. And, thanks to the photo in the locket, he already had his next mark.

A nudge against his calf brought the man out of his reverie. He looked down at the cat, which was up to its usual trick of weaving between his legs, rubbing its flanks against his calves, but never allowing itself to be stroked. When it was done, it sat close by, staring intently up at him. The two locked eyes for a long moment.

The man finished his pint and was about to get up when the animal leapt on his lap, turned around as though it were about to lie down for a snooze, rubbing itself against the man's chest as it did so, and then was gone – jumping down before the man could react and disappearing into the darkness by the side of the bar.

~

Officers from the Metropolitan Police Service's Homicide and Major Crime Command had been watching the man for a while. The CCTV cameras near the school of the teenage victim had captured him several times walking on the opposite side of the road. There was no crime against walking in the street, but when the broken body of the girl was eventually found by police divers, the officer in charge of the investigation decided to take a chance and pay a visit to the man's West London home, along with his sergeant.

"Do you have any pets, sir?" asked Detective Chief Inspector Harrison, surreptitiously placing in his pocket the animal hair he'd spotted clinging to a jacket hanging over the back of a chair in the man's sitting-room.

"No." The man was genuinely surprised. "No, I don't... Why d'you ask?"

"No reason, sir. I just noticed some animal hair on your jacket there."

"Ah, I see," the man smiled, relaxing into the sofa. "It must be the cat from the pub. It's all over me whenever I go in." DCI Harrison smiled and nodded. Reassured that there was nothing sinister behind the question, the man ventured a little joke, "Cats can tell who's good and who's bad, you know, Chief Inspector, so I must be a very good man... But seriously, I'm afraid I really can't help you. I hope you catch who did it, though."

"You mentioned a pub..." DCI Harrison wasn't going to let it go. One of the few surviving pieces of DNA evidence, given the state of decomposition of the girl's body after weeks in a bag in a canal, were a couple of sandy-coloured cat hairs that had been removed from the girl's hair and from the inside of the bag. And neither the girl's family, nor apparently anyone she knew, owned a cat with matching fur.

The man paused for moment, weighing up his options. He couldn't pretend that he'd forgotten the name of the pub because he'd already let the cat out the bag, as it were, by indicating that he'd been there more than once. If he gave the name of another pub and the police checked it out, they wouldn't find a cat in it and they'd wonder why he'd lied. If he gave them the right name, what was the worst that could happen? There was nothing linking any of the girls to the pub, and the police would see that he wasn't lying.

"*The Organ Grinder,*" he finally said, adding casually in a bid to appear helpful: "It's just the other side of Southfield Green. Kind of a spooky old place, but quiet enough of an evening."

While waiting for the lab results to come in, DCI Harrison decided to go for a pint at *The Organ Grinder*. He was surprised he'd never come across the pub before. Then again, who'd want to drink in a pub painted entirely black on the exterior, and with lighting that hardly penetrated the creeping shadows inside?

"How can I help you?" the tired, sad-looking woman at the bar gazed at DCI Harrison with little enthusiasm.

"I'm DCI Harrison with the Metropolitan Police. I'd be grateful if you could take a look at this photo and tell me if you've seen this man before." He held out a photo of the man he'd recently visited.

"Yes," the woman behind the bar replied. "I first noticed him a few months ago and since then he's become something of a regular. Has something happened to him?"

"Just routine questions, madam," said Harrison. "You must have a lot of customers. How come you remember him so well?"

"It's a funny thing. There's a cat that hangs around the pub. I feed it sometimes, but it never lets me get anywhere near it. Or anybody else for that matter. Except for that man. Whenever he comes in, the cat's all over him."

"You mean he's the only one that can stroke it?"

"Not exactly. I mean, it follows him around everywhere, pesters him, even jumps on him. But I don't think he's ever actually managed to stroke it."

As DCI Harrison left *The Organ Grinder*, he thought he caught sight of a pair of green-flecked amber eyes glowing in the shadows under one of the tables. But when he looked closer, they were gone.

~

"*Felis silvestris lybica*. It's your African wildcat again." The forensics specialist looked distinctly pleased with himself. "This time I was prepared." The first time Harrison had brought him a couple of animal hairs – recovered from the body of the murdered girl – he'd had to consult with an American colleague and do a global database search, as the feline they came from didn't match anything native to Britain. A search of public and private zoos hadn't unearthed any missing stock, and there was no such animal listed on any veterinary database either.

"Thanks!" DCI Harrison headed swiftly for the door, convinced now that the man marked by the cat hair was the sick bastard he was after. Now he'd have to do everything by the book: get a search warrant, *Miranda* the man, help the Crown Prosecutor build a strong case.

"Detective Chief Inspector!" the forensics expert stopped Harrison for a moment. "You caught me by surprise last time, so I did a little reading. Most of our moggies are descended from the African wildcat, you know. But your cat is the real deal – they still live in the wild in Africa and the Middle East. In the past some of them chose to live with people because they could prey on rodents attracted by grain stores. They've been known to kills snakes and scorpions so the Ancient Egyptians believed they could vanquish evil."

~

A year had passed since the successful prosecution and incarceration of the girl's killer. The cat with fur the colour of the desert, dubbed *Monster* by the barwoman – in revenge for the fact that it took the food she offered, but refused to come anywhere near her – continued to skulk around *The Organ Grinder*, startling the occasional punter with its silent footfall and soul-penetrating stare.

It was a surprisingly warm day in early March, when rays of the afternoon sun had somehow managed to invade the less gloomy corners of *The Organ Grinder*, and a small group of delivery boys from the local pizza parlour who had just finished their shift were playing a round of pool on the newly installed table.

The cat, which had been hiding in some spot of the pub known only to itself, appeared suddenly by the entrance door, ears alert, and quivering from whiskers to tail. A moment later the door opened, and a tall, attractive brunette, well dressed and wearing large sunglasses, strode confidently in. Her sights were set on one of the young men playing pool; she'd singled him out for her own special brand of 'cat and mouse', and she certainly wouldn't be assuming the role of *mus musculus*. She'd buy herself a drink and watch him for a while from a table that remained bathed in darkness despite the brightness of the day.

But first she had to shake the strange-looking cat that was rubbing itself against her legs and leaving pale-coloured hairs all over her black lace stockings.

Also by Anna Taborska:

Novels

Tales from the Organ Grinder (Forthcoming)

Collections

For Those Who Dream Monsters (Mortbury Press, 2013)

Bloody Britain (Shadow Publishing, TBC)

Visit Anna Taborska at her website:
annataborska.wixsite.com/horror

Now available and forthcoming from
Black Shuck Shadows:

Shadows 1 – The Spirits of Christmas
by Paul Kane

Shadows 2 – Tales of New Mexico
by Joseph D'Lacey

Shadows 3 – Unquiet Waters
by Thana Niveau

Shadows 4 – The Life Cycle
by Paul Kane

Shadows 5 – The Death of Boys
by Gary Fry

Shadows 6 – Broken on the Inside
by Phil Sloman

Shadows 7 – The Martledge Variations
by Simon Kurt Unsworth

Shadows 8 – Singing Back the Dark
by Simon Bestwick

blackshuckbooks.co.uk/shadows

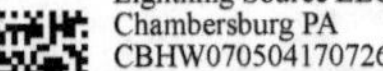